MORO

Patricia Eckenrod

Second Edition

Copyright © 2026

Translated by Sandra Giroux
Arcane Book Design
ISBN: 979-8-9955168-1-1
Second Edition — 2026

Published by Linguamia Press

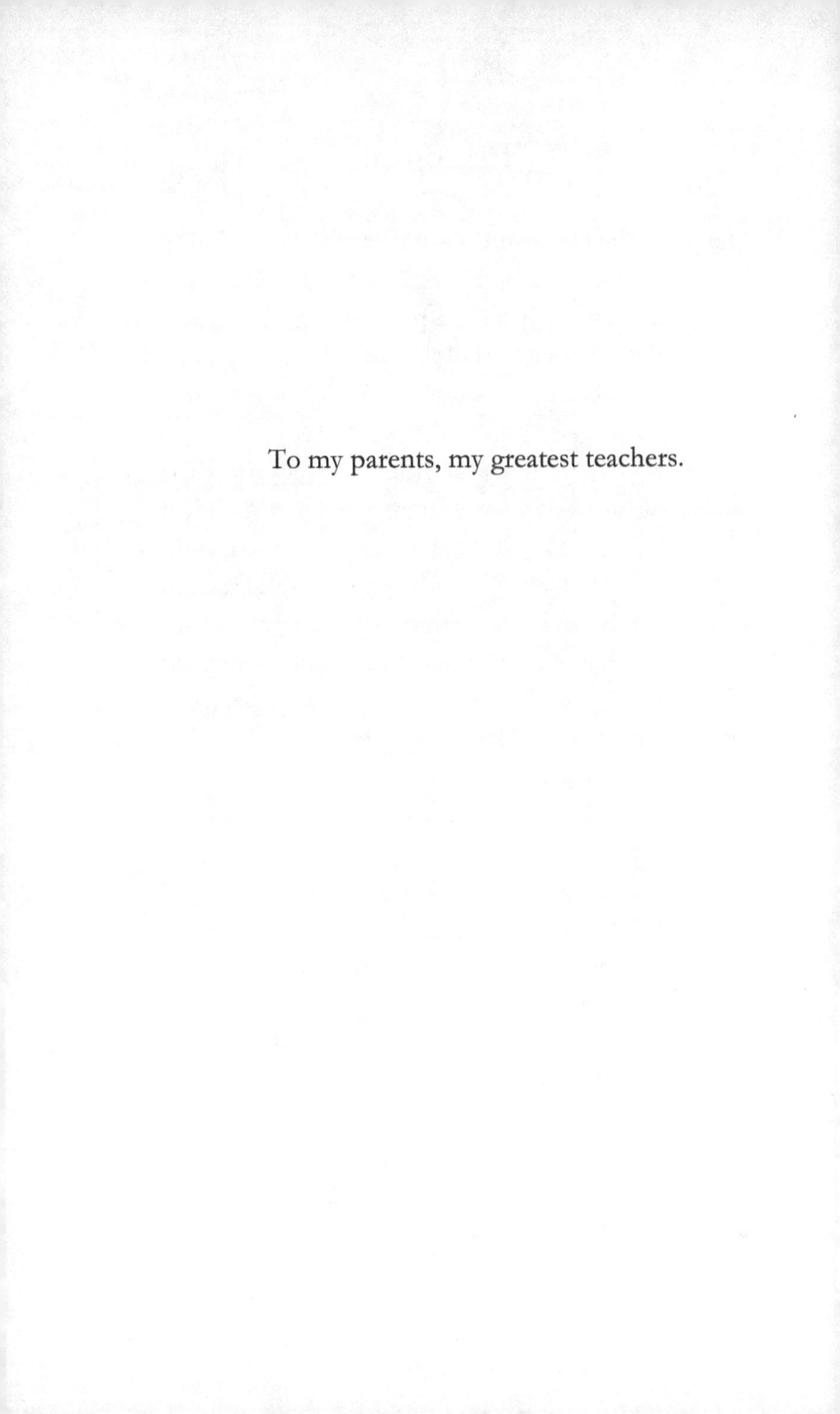

To my parents, my greatest teachers.

Prologue

This story began to unfold many years ago, during my childhood, when my father brought home a small, charming colt whose presence would change our lives. He named him Moro, after the deep, dusky color of his coat.

Each line of this story blends reality with the fantasy of joyful days spent in an ideal world — just my father, Pequeño, and me. Though we were eight siblings, the others had already grown up and moved away. Getting back to… this was a dreamlike chapter, a time when we ran freely through fields stitched with poetry — our spirits lifted by the wind, learning from our parents and from life itself.

From the moment Moro entered our lives, he became more than a colt — he became Pequeño's closest friend. Their bond was instinctive, joyful, and pure. My little brother often searched the pastures for Moro, who wandered off to be near the mares. When he found him, Moro would gallop toward him, neighing with joy, his mane dancing in the breeze, and his teeth bared in a wide, delighted grin.

Pequeño sometimes tried to trick him — pretending to hold salt in one hand while hiding a rope in the other. But Moro was too clever to be fooled.

He didn't come for the salt; he came for the boy he loved. Even when it meant leaving the comfort of the herd, he would choose friendship over freedom. Moro was happiest at Pequeño's side. His loyalty was unwavering; his friendship was deeper than words — a kind of love that outshone even the most devoted human love.

The lessons I learned from my parents during those years deeply shaped me. Their quiet, steady wisdom became the foundation of who I am. But it was Moro's strength, courage, and gentle heart that stirred something even more — a creative spark long buried beneath the dust of forgotten memories. Writing about him became a way to recover what time had hidden and to listen again to the whispers of those magical days.

I always believed my brother would one day not only paint Moro, capturing his spirit in color and form, but also tell this story, brush in hand, heart wide open. But life had other plans. So I took the liberty of telling his story — not just for my father and brother, but for the little girl I once was, who ran through fields with a colt and a dream.

Now Moro not only lives in my memory but also in the hearts of those who hear his story. He embodies the essence of true friendship and the quiet wisdom passed down by his teacher and companion, Don Felipe.

This is his story:

1

The Beginning of a Great Friendship

I'm not sure how to start my story. I wasn't born to be a writer, and I don't think anyone like me has ever been one — at least not that I know of. So I'll begin by writing from my heart. As I recall these memories — those intangible threads we call time — I'll fill these pages with the stories that live inside me.

Sometimes in school vacations, the little boy — Pequeño, whose real name was Hernan — would wake early and run to the pasture where we grazed. He was eight years old, the youngest of eight siblings, and everyone called him Pequeño because of his size, though his spirit was anything but small.

As soon as he arrived, he would shout with joy.

"Moro! Blanco! Let's have some fun! Estelita is waiting for us!" he told us.

Estelita was his sister, two years older than him.

"Let's go! Let's gallop!" He was repeatedly excited as he climbed onto my back, and Blanco would follow close behind. Together, we raced toward home, where Estelita waited with eager eyes. Once she mounted Blanco, the adventure began.

"Faster, faster, faster!" they cheered, gripping our manes and pressing their legs against our sides, urging us forward with laughter and delight.

We galloped with abandon, the wind rushing past and our hooves pounding the earth like a drumbeat of joy.

"Let's go that way", Estelita gestured.

"No, no, let's go the other way... past the orange and tangerine groves!" Pequeño pointed, and we took off in that direction.

At other times, we went by the banana plantations. No matter the route, the journey was always filled with laughter and wonder.

They loved searching for fallen nests, gently returning fragile baby birds to the nest, their small hands cradling life with reverence. The world felt enchanted then — every leaf, every breeze, every gallop a celebration of freedom.

I remember once, as the sun was ascending on the horizon, lighting up that seemingly endless landscape. Everything danced. The trees swayed rhythmically in the breeze, carrying the scent of wildflowers, field grass, and orange blossoms.

"Ha, ha, ha, ha!" The laughter of the two children was perfectly timed with the beat of our hooves. We moved so swiftly it felt as if we were flying, weightless and wild.

My chest swelled with energy; my muzzle half–open to play in the wind. We raced as if we owned the world and time, with savage freedom, unrestrained. We flew over the fields, leaping over fallen trunks, unsaddled and unfettered. The kids clung to our manes. Blood pulsed through us with such vitality, and we cried out in joy. Our manes danced in the breeze. When we finally tired, wrapped in a fascinating bubble, we headed home, breathless and ecstatic.

Then we went down toward the river, splashing into the water and making waves, and the fun kept rolling. Woo–hoo! That was living.

2

My Encounter with My Owner

One of my most vivid memories is the look in my owner's eyes. His light brown hazel eyes reminded me of honey—warm, golden, and full of quiet kindness. His freckled face, dotted like overripe bananas, held the softness of someone who had lived gently. His hair shimmered with the fiery hues of a sunset, as if the sky itself had settled in his head.

I remembered it was early that morning. The world felt different. The sun rose, casting long shadows and bathing the earth in a golden hush. It wasn't an ordinary day. Life itself had a welcome surprise for me.

Don Felipe, my new owner, pulled a handful of bills from his pocket and handed them to the man who had owned me. I was happy then. I don't know why. Maybe I had a sad memory from the past, but I didn't remember what it was.

And then, with that quiet exchange, I belonged to Don Felipe.

Before we began our journey, he looked into my eyes and smiled, and that smile seemed to reach deep into my soul. He gently placed a rope around my neck and said, "I will name you Moro. That's a lovely name for you." He was so close that I could see my own face shimmering in his eyes — small, unsure, yet full of hope. My heart stirred with a quiet thrill. What I felt was beyond words. When I finally surfaced from that spell, one thought rose in me: how lucky I was to be beside him. I said this because, since that moment, something in me had stayed close, gentle, and unmistakably near him. And I like my name, I thought. It suits me.

From that moment on, I was Moro, and I was his.

We began our journey together. In that moment, I looked around, as if seeing the world for the first time. Everything was so beautiful, bright, and fragrant.

I walked slowly, pulled by a rope. I don't remember my parents or where I came from. I don't know the herd I came from or the place where I was born. I only remember him — the man who gave me love, cherished me like a friend and a brother, and gave me a name and, with it, a place in the world.

We walked for hours, seventy kilometers or more, through a landscape that unfolded like a dream. The sun climbed higher, crowding the earth with light. Coffee berries ripened for harvest, cacao pods perfumed the air, and almond trees cast long shadows across the path. Mangoes and oranges glowed in the orchards, and the pasture stretched endlessly around us.

Above us, flocks of birds soared in synchronized flight. Cars sped past on the nearby road, their engines roaring like distant thunder, leaving clouds of dust that blurred my vision and filled my ears with a buzzing hum.

I was not used to walking long distances. It felt like an eternity.

We walked a few more steps, searching for shade. We were hungry and tired. Finally, Don Felipe found a great acacia tree. He stopped, hugged me, and laughed softly.

"Well, the river brought us this far, Moro," he said, his voice full of warmth and lightheartedness. "This is as far as we've come today." I mean to say — you must take life lightly — he told me, laughing again.

Something inside me stirred — a feeling I couldn't quite name. A tear welled in my eyes as he caressed my neck. No one had ever touched me like that before. No one had ever seen me like he did.

He sat beneath the acacia tree, and I stood nearby, watching the world shimmer around us. Then he looked at me and said:

"Moro, you're one of a kind. I had never seen a more beautiful colt."

I didn't understand the words, but they sounded like music.

"I have another horse at home," my owner said softly, his voice full of affection. "You'll meet him soon. I'm sure you'll become good friends. His name is Blanco — meaning 'white' — because his coat is as pure as ermine. He's strong and handsome. But you, Moro… you're something else. Young, yes — but special."

"Wow!" I thought, my heart fluttering. I was beginning to understand the sweetness of his words.

We paused beneath the leafy canopy of that acacia tree, taking a moment to rest in that beautiful spot. The air was alive with birdsong, its melody weaving through the branches above a field of wild-flowers that spread like a painted dream. I stood quietly, absorbing the colors, the scents, and the feeling of being seen.

After a while, my owner rose and smiled.

"Shall we go on?"

We kept moving forward, leaving behind the sights I was experiencing for the very first time — moments I knew I would carry with me always.

As we walked, the sun began to set, its golden light fading into soft lavender and rose. The sky darkened slowly until the moon appeared — suspended like a lantern in the vastness above. Lamps flickered in the countryside we passed, casting warm light through windows and across porches.

"This is as far as we'll go," he said. "Let's ask for shelter."

He knocked gently on the door. A humble elderly woman opened it, her face kind and weathered.

"This colt and I are looking for a place to stay tonight," he said. "May we stay here?"

She nodded with a gentle smile and beckoned him inside. He thanked her sincerely, his gratitude as genuine as the moon rising above us.

(What a time that was — when people welcomed strangers into their homes without fear, only with kindness.)

After the long walk on scorching asphalt, my hooves were burned, and the sun was so hot that it left me drenched in sweat, overheated, and exhausted.

While he slept inside, I spent the night beneath a small roof attached to the cottage. It felt as if all the silver in the universe had melted across the landscape, casting its glow on the trees, the grass, and everything beneath the moon's watchful eye. Crickets chirped and hopped around my legs. Not far off, I heard the soft murmur of a river flowing between a bamboo grove and a weeping willow, its voice gentle and eternal.

I closed my eyes, and the night's sounds faded into silence. I drifted into sleep, wrapped in peace.

At dawn, I woke up to the music of morning birds chirping overhead, their wings fluttering in the light. A rooster crowed repeatedly, announcing the start of a new day. The scent of dew drifted on the breeze, and nearby, a fruit seller rang a bell, offering his harvest to the waking world.

Animals stirred around me, stepping into the sunlight with quiet joy. I nibbled on fresh grass and discovered green plantains — sweet and soft, a new delight. Then I saw him, my owner, walking toward me, adjusting his hat.

His presence filled me with warmth. I felt safe, seen, and loved. As I finished the last bite of the plantains, he patted my head gently, then secured the rope around my neck while I rested my head on his shoulder.

"Did you sleep well, Moro? Are you ready to continue our journey?"

His concern stirred something tender in me. I nodded, baring my teeth in a wide grin and snorting in agreement.

"Today, we'll go slower than yesterday. I don't want your little hooves to get hurt. We'll stop somewhere to splash in the water."

How sweet — he cared about my hooves, too. The thought of water made me hopeful.

We set out again, the morning air cool against our skin. The sky above was a bright blue, with clouds drifting like wisps of tulle. My owner led me gently, and we continued our way.

"Moro! You look like a racehorse," he said proudly.

His words lifted my spirits. I felt a flicker of equine vanity and a quiet joy at being seen.

We kept walking until nearly noon. The sun came back with its blazing heat, and the asphalt shimmered with warmth. I started to feel faint from the humidity, quietly wishing for the promised break.

Then, as if called by my thoughts, a gentle sound reached us — the murmur of flowing water. A cool breeze brushed my face.

"A stream!" he exclaimed.

We followed the sound and turned toward it. There, we discovered a hidden creek, tucked away like a secret of crystal-clear water.

Relief flooded over me.

Here, we can quench our thirst and refresh our-selves.

The sun blazed overhead like a brazier, and he joked that we were well — roasted chickens. I agreed wholeheartedly.

An almond tree gracefully curved over the path, its leaves whispering in the breeze. I moved forward, stepped into the creek, and lowered my head to drink deeply. The water was cold and sweet, and I drank as if I might never stop.

"You were very thirsty, Moro. You nearly dried up the creek," he teased.

I neighed and looked at him, amused. He crouched by the water, cupping his hands to drink. He's the one who nearly dried it up, I thought, whin-nying softly. I considered nudging him into the wa-ter, but held back — I was still a colt, and he was an adult. That kind of play would come later, maybe.

Then he splashed me, and I jumped in beside him. He scooped water over my body with a coconut shell he'd found, and I danced in the stream, sending waves in every direction. He dove in, and after his bath, we climbed out and rested.

He leaned against the almond tree, and I wandered nearby, watching butterflies flutter like petals in the wind. A frog sat on a lily pad, gazing at me, blinking slowly, as if meditating. The bamboo grove swayed gently, its rustling leaves harmonizing with the stream's song.

He ate some yuca bread while I nibbled on grass. Our hunger eased, and the quiet place, with nature's symphony, lulled us. I think he dozed off for a while. When he woke up, he stretched and said:

"Well, we're rested now. Time to get moving."

He grabbed the rope, and we continued. I glanced back to say goodbye to the frog, but he had vanished.

The sun still burned, but the heat began to ease. We walked until sundown, slowing as fatigue crept in. I was too tired to admire the scenery, but my owner noticed and encouraged me:

"Come on, Moro, you got this! We're nearly there!"

A few more steps and then,

"Look over there! We're here at last, Moro!"

I lifted my head. A small town appeared before us, nestled in the golden light of the evening. Relief surged through me. We had arrived.

The sky shimmered in purple and gold, a fleeting universe of color. Birds danced in the air, and I felt as if I were dreaming. The town was quiet, with only a few houses, their balconies adorned with pink roses and red geraniums. A nearby river flowed gently, guiding us toward his home.

We climbed a small hill to reach a vantage point.

"Look!" he said, pointing to a house nestled among trees.

We descended into a cozy meadow, and there it was — his home.

"Here it is! This will be your home, Moro!"

The house stood on a corner, surrounded by lush grass and enclosed by a wooden fence.

Bougainvillea spilled over the walls in vibrant, cascading splendor. As soon as he opened the gate, I admired how the garden was alive with hydrangeas, hibiscus, basil, lemongrass, and melissa, their fragrance lingering in the air.

He opened the gate and welcomed me in.

"Come this way, Moro," he said, guiding me toward a majestic avocado tree.

The breeze carried the scents of flowers and fruits. I felt safe. I felt joy. I felt the warmth of his home.

"Come out, kids! We're home!" he called. And then — I heard them. Footsteps, fast and eager, rushing toward him like a squad.

3

His Family, My Family

They came running all at once, like a joyful stampede. The first I noticed was the youngest — Pequeño. His eyes sparkled with curiosity, and his straight, dark brown hair bounced as he ran. He stopped in front of me, breathless and beaming.

And gazing at me, he flashed a big smile.

"What a cute horse you are! Unlike any other!" he said, his voice full of wonder.

"Hi, Papa! What's the little foal's name?"

"Moro," my owner replied.

"Moro?" replied Pequeño.

"Hello, Moro! What a cute little horse you are!" Pequeño repeated, standing on tiptoe to gently pat my neck.

Later, I learned he oversaw bathing and saddling Blanco whenever my owner was away. He had a deep love for animals, and from that moment, I knew we'd be great friends.

Then a little girl with long hair tied in a ponytail
– just like mine — came. She greeted my owner with
a cheerful:

"Hi, Dad!"
Before he could respond, she turned to me and
exclaimed:
"Hi, little horse… I mean, Moro! You're so
cute!"
She reached up to stroke my neck, then paused,
gazing thoughtfully.

"Moro! Like rice and lentils, right, Dad?"
"That's right!" he answered.
It's a beautiful and delicious name, and every-
body laughed.

Her name was Estelita. She had a bright smile
and a voice … well, I later discovered, often sounded
like a broody hen's when she sang. Every morning,
she fed the chickens with great care.

Finally, another — a teenage girl with long, light
hair tied back. She glanced at me, shrugged, and
walked away without a word.
"Ah! It's just a little horse," she muttered.
Leaving me surprised.

My equine vanity, used to being called "cute" and "special," wilted a little. But I reminded myself: praise is just an opinion, not a truth. Not everyone will agree.

Then I saw her — she was Doña Felicia, my master's wife — a woman with a gentle gaze, a lovely face, slender and petite, generous in the quiet way of those who give without thinking.

She didn't reach out to touch me, yet her eyes rested on me with tender warmth as she murmured.

"What a beautiful colt... he must be weary from so much walking." Then, with the gentle tone of someone who cares for all living things, she added, "Let Pequeño fetch the grass; let him rest instead of walking all the way to the pasture."

I immediately liked her.

Just then, a pig came sniffing around the yard. I learned his name was Pancho. Two red hens fluttered out of the bushes, landing near my feet and clucking excitedly. A large rooster followed, stopping abruptly when he saw me. He tilted his head, stared, then puffed out his chest and declared:

"Even though you're big and good-looking, I am the king here!"

I blinked in surprise. What an odd welcome, I thought, snorting softly.

A wrinkly iguana crept along a branch of the avocado tree, staring at me with wide eyes. Below, a turtle emerged from the shade, listening to the rooster's boast. She moved slowly toward him and said:

"Giro, don't be so insecure. You can proclaim yourself the king of the henhouse, but not all of us. If anyone's our king, it's Don Felipe. He cares for us. He protects us. He loves us."

Then she turned to me, her eyes kind and steady.

"Welcome, Moro."

Oh… Good thing! I have an advocate, I thought, amused and grateful. I snorted gently.

"Hello, lady turtle."

"Linda. My name is Linda," she replied, sensing my hesitation.

How kind she is, I thought, touched by her warmth.

"Thanks," I snorted again, meeting her gaze. She gave a friendly glance, then slowly walked away. The rooster strutted off, swinging his red crest proudly.

4

Moro's First Night in His New Home

The sun was sinking slowly, and the first shadows of dusk were spreading across the land. The girls went inside; Pequeño went to gather the grass for me.

My master unsaddled me and said:

"Before darkness settles in, he said softly, "and while Pequeño brings your grass, let's go for a bath." As he gently touched my haunch, he guided me toward a small river, which flowed through the back of the house.

A gentle slope led us downward, and even before reaching the edge, I heard the soft murmur of flowing water. The path was lined with lush, dense vegetation — trees of various kinds, vines that curled like dancers, Camacho plants, bijou plants, and other exotic wonders that flirted with the river's current. A small waterfall spilled onto the ground nearby, its crystal stream crashing with joyful force, awakening my senses.

In that river, I took my first bath in my new home.

My owner poured buckets of water over my hot body, each splash falling like a cool, refreshing wave. I snorted and playfully splashed him back with my snout. We laughed — well, he laughed, and I neighed with delight. We played like children. I felt like one, and in those moments, he did too. His laughter was light, unburdened, and I saw in him the joy of a boy rediscovering wonder.

As the day's colors faded into twilight, he brushed my mane with a long brush, each stroke calming and rhythmic. My stomach growled, eager for the grass Pequeño had promised. As I hoped, my little friend arrived, arms full of freshly cut greens, his smile as generous as the bundle he carried.

That night, after the curtain of dusk had fallen, I looked up at the sky as dark as my past. Then a single star twinkled into view. Another followed. And yet another. Before long, the night was filled with a tapestry of stars, the most beautiful starry night I had ever seen.

The stars shimmered and danced, their reflections captured in my eyes, like mirrors of my young, joyful heart — unclouded, untroubled, free.

I listened to the wind's whisper, the river's lullaby, the rustling leaves, the chirping crickets, and the silent dance of fireflies glowing softly in the dark. I lay down in wonder, surrounded by the scents of flowers, herbs, and earth. The house grew quiet. Lights dimmed. Windows closed. Silence settled over me like a warm blanket.

And in that peaceful moment, I drifted off to sleep in the most serene place I had ever imagined.

5

Moro Meeting Blanco

At dawn, the chickens gathered in a flurry, followed by the distant ringing of bells, like echoes of a dream. I woke happy and refreshed, as if the past had disappeared overnight. It felt as if my life truly began the day my owner found me.

I got up and stretched, eager for the gift of a new day. The sun rose, its golden rays spread across the landscape, turning the sky a vivid blue. The morning came alive with sounds — rustling leaves, chirping birds, and the gentle hum of awakening life.

Estelita was already feeding the hens, her eyes gentle as she watched the fluffy chicks peck and wobble. Giro, the rooster, strutted among them, pecking at the grass proudly. He gave me a disdainful look and then turned away, unimpressed.

I looked up and saw the wrinkled iguana staring at me with her bulging eyes. She slowly climbed down, with Linda waiting below the canopy. When Verde reached the ground, she turned to Linda and muttered:

"Look at that arrogant colt. He thinks he's special."

"Why do you say that, Verde?" Linda asked gently. "He doesn't see himself as special. But he is," she added softly, with conviction. "Envy isn't a positive feeling. Like Moro, you are also beautiful, with an emerald-like glow. Everybody is unique in their own way."

Verde blinked, and her tone softened.
"That's true," she admitted. Her voice was steadier than Giro's.

Her words didn't really lift my mood, but they quickly disappeared as birds started singing from the avocado tree, their songs blending seamlessly through the branches.

Then I saw him — my owner — step out of the house in his work clothes, rope in hand.

He walked toward me with a smile that warmed the morning air.

"Hi, Moro! Did you sleep well? Of course you did — under the stars," he said with a chuckle after answering his own question. "You know, when I was a kid, I would stare at the stars and feel like I could reach out and grab a handful. But as we grow older, we forget how magical it is to be a child."

He gently wrapped the rope around my neck. "We are heading to the pasture to see Blanco." I whinnied, showing my big teeth, and he laughed as we began our walk.

We walked along a clear path, leaving the house behind us—flanked by trees and lush plants in all shades of green. My owner had a natural talent for making friends; his laughter was infectious, and wherever we went, people welcomed him with respect and happiness.

"Hello, Don Felipe!"

"Look, this is my little foal, Moro!" he'd reply, beaming.

"Beautiful colt!"

Soon, we came to a cornfield swaying softly in the breeze. It was the first I had ever seen.

"Be careful not to brush against the leaves of corn plants. Sometimes there are worms on them called *pachones*. They are very poisonous," he warned me.

I walked on with every sense awake, my gaze drifting over the rows as if the whole field were holding its breath. I tried not to touch the leaves, but the rough stalks still scraped softly against me, crackling like dry paper in the heat. Now and then, a loose silk brushed my neck — a pale golden thread, light as a whisper, like the corn's own hair reaching out to graze me as I passed.

A breeze swept through, whistling in the sunlight. The corn stalks stood like soldiers at attention, and I felt a thrill as we walked along a narrow path across the field.

Then my owner pointed ahead.

"Look, That's Blanco!"

A beautiful white horse stood nearby, grazing peacefully. Its tail moved gently, and its mane sparkled in the morning sunlight. It seemed almost otherworldly — like something out of a dream. I wasn't sure what angel horses look like, but I imagined they must resemble him.

"Isn't he beautiful? He's a good horse, too."

We moved forward slowly. The sunlight illuminated Blanco brilliantly, and beyond him, the fields extended endlessly, a vast sea of green.

"Hello, my dear Blanco!" my owner said, embracing him.

"This is Moro. He's part of our family now."

He turned to me.

This is Blanco, the horse I mentioned earlier.

Blanco and I exchanged a meaningful glance, as if our souls connected. While meeting his children was delightful, encountering Blanco evoked a deeper sense of kinship.

"Hi, Moro! Welcome," Blanco neighed softly.
"Hi, Blanco. Thank you!" I replied, baring my teeth in a wide smile.

We touched noses, and my owner waved goodbye, leaving us together.

From that moment forward, we were inseparable. We strolled under the stars, crossed rivers and roads, explored woodlands, and admired nature's beauty. No matter how much time passes, we never get tired of each other. We jumped fences, pursued adventures, and experienced together the happiness and sadness that life had prepared for us.

I grew up learning from Blanco; he was my guide, my friend, my brother. And together, we listened to the stories the earth whispered to us day by day.

6

Memories

Time passed, and my mind became a garden of memories. In quiet moments, lying on the grass beside Blanco, far from the bustle of town, I would gaze at the starry sky I love so deeply. I remember how one star would appear, then another, and another — until the vast heavens shimmered with light. It felt as though their glow had entered me, leaving behind a brilliance that settled in my eyes.

On nights with a full moon, its silver glow shone through the leaves, creating moving patterns on the forest floor in the quiet of the night. The air was filled with frogs croaking, leaves rustling, and the gentle movement of hidden creatures — a natural symphony that eased me into calmness.

At dawn each day, the birds sang sweet melodies that drifted through the trees. Sometimes Blanco and I chased after hummingbirds, though I never managed to catch one; we had fun. I watched in awe as they hovered, fragile and quick, sipping nectar from the flower's calyx like tiny dancers lost in a dream.

During winter, Blanco and I would race to seek shelter from the heavy rains, splashing through puddles as we galloped. I also loved every sunset that sank into my existence, much like I enjoyed the start and finish of spring. We ran with the children through fields, gathering ripe, juicy fruits to quell our hunger, laughing under the golden sunlight.

These touching moments are forever etched in my memory. Words can't fully express the joy I experienced with my owner, his two youngest children, and Blanco. Besides, I learned that we were part of something whole. We share the same origins, the same breath of life. We were connected.

Back then, I grew — not just in size, but in spirit. I was no longer a colt. I had become a *cimarron*. Though the word often refers to a wild horse, to me it symbolizes something else: a transformation. I had stepped into a new world. The little Moro had vanished, and in his place stood an impetuous horse, filled with determination, curiosity, and fire.

A new sensation arose within me, something I had never experienced before. I began to admire the mares grazing in the nearby pastures along our trails. Each day, I envisioned a different one. In my mind, they all seemed drawn to me — and they truly were. They called me handsome and a good horse. I didn't quite understand why, but I felt proud as I walked those familiar paths with my head held high.

It was around that time that my owner decided to take us — Blanco, the two children, and me — to a beautiful jungle region he said we would love. A place of wonder. A place where new memories would bloom.

7
My Owner's Paradise

The night before our trip to the jungle, I was filled with restless excitement. Sleep eluded me as heavy rain pounded the earth, tapping against the roof like a thousand galloping horses. Lightning lit up the sky with dazzling flashes, making my heart race, while thunder roared so loudly it seemed to shake my ears and bones. I waited impatiently for the storm to pass and for dawn to break. Finally, the rain eased, and I heard the familiar "cock – a doodle – doo" echoing through the mist — a sign that morning had arrived.

Even though the sun had just begun to rise, the house was lively with activity. Everyone prepped eagerly for the highly anticipated trip. Pequeño and Blanco, experienced travelers, discussed the jungle as if it were a magical, enchanted land. For Estelita and me, it was a new adventure, filled with mysteries waiting to be uncovered.

Don Felipe and Pequeño came out first, saddlebags and backpacks in hand. They carefully saddled us, checking every strap and buckle. My owner loaded food and essentials into the bags and secured them to our backs. Estelita arrived soon after, her backpack slung over her shoulders and her hat snug on her head.

"All set?" he asked.

"Yes, Dad," she replied.

"We need to hurry before it gets as hot as an oven out there. Come on, what are you waiting for?" he teased the children. "And don't forget the mosquito repellent and the mosquito net — jungle anopheles love fresh blood, and they are very aggressive because they transmit malaria. We've got to be careful."

"Everything's ready," his wife called out. She was always on top of things.

"Come on, I'll help you get on Moro," he said, lifting Estelita onto my back.

I didn't understand why he chose her to ride me. She usually preferred Blanco — calm, gentle, predictable. I was different. Unruly. Especially when I saw a mare. The sight of a female made me wild — I'd rear up, paw the air, trying to impress, heedless of the consequences. I would never harm Estelita, but she didn't know that. Perhaps she was afraid that a mare might appear along the path and that I would erupt into a wild, uncontrollable, bravado. Even so, she remained seated upon my back, waiting with a patient stillness.

My owner then helped Pequeño onto Blanco's back. And now, at last, we opened the door to adventure and began to walk. Our hoofbeats echoed with every step we took on the damp earth. The air was beginning to warm, and insects stirred now and then after a night of rain. My owner, silent, walked beside us; after taking a few steps, he asked us:

"How did you sleep, guys?"

"I couldn't close my eyes," Estelita said, weary. "The thunder and lightning kept me awake. I just wanted the morning to come, but the rain on the roof made time drag on forever."

"I felt the same," Pequeño added. "I lay awake, listening to the storm and fearing the thunder that hammered, hammered, hammered above the roof."

I felt as if I had been nothing more than a spectator the night before, watching a storm of thunder and lightning unfold on a stage, wanting to explain everything I had felt and heard. But lacking the skill to do so, I only shook my head and let out a snort that no one paid any attention to.

"Yes, it rained cats and dogs last night," my owner said. "Nothing feels longer than waiting for something you're excited about. But look — we're on our way now."

Blanco, familiar with the road, led the way. I followed, watching the saddlebags sway with each step and Blanco's tail wagging gently. The sunrise painted the horizon in warm golden hues, and although the ground was wet, we kept going along the path.

"The road is slippery," my owner said, "but it doesn't matter. You'll see wonders ahead."

Our faces lit up with excitement. I felt eager, proud, elegant, and admired. Blanco remained calm, yet he walked with a steady pace. We journeyed through the center of the small town, where green foliage shimmered under a clear sky. My owner's reddish-gold hair shone in the sunlight, and he glanced at us now and then to make sure we were all right.

We turned right onto the road that would lead us to the enchanting place.

The air was heavy with humidity; we could hear the lowing of cows, the barking of dogs, and the clucking of hens as we passed the houses that lined the edges of the farms.

We moved slowly, walking carefully, slipping now and then. We hadn't gone far when we reached a place called El Barro Colorado. It was named for the reddish clay soil that turned into a quagmire whenever it rained. Now the road had become a river of mud, so much so that even Blanco and I struggled to walk. With every step, one hoof sank deeply; we pulled it out with effort, only to get stuck with the other. That stretch of road was a challenge; even so, we managed to get through with Estelita and Pequeño on our backs.

My owner walked along the edge of the mire, boots in hand, struggling through the mud just as we were.

At last, we made it through the swamp and stepped onto solid ground. We continued along the path, marveling at the lush landscape around us. Tall, magnificent trees lined the way. The air lingered with the scent of damp earth, mingled with the fragrance of wildflowers and untamed plants.

I was lost in my own contemplation when we heard a sound like a river roaring with great force; it grew louder as we approached. We saw that it was a river overflowing its banks. The current surged with fierce momentum; the water was a churning mix of mud and river water, and on its surface floated a massive tangle of debris-branches, sticks, and grass blocking the river's flow. The storm from the night before had not only washed the land clean; it had also caused the river to overflow, and the wooden bridge had collapsed... There was no way across.

My owner stood still, thoughtful. I knew that look. He was brave and resolute. We would find a way.

"Dad, we're going back, right?" Estelita asked, her voice trembling. "We're not going to cross, are we?"

"Of course we are."

"But how?"

"We can't fly," he said with a playful smile. He spread his arms wide, like wings, and added, "And with this sun and heat, our wings would melt — just like Icarus' did." He winked. "You know, the boy from Greek mythology who flew too close to the sun with wings made of wax and feathers." Since we can't fly, we can use our arms to swim.

"But the river is overflowing! I don't think we can cross it!" she insisted, distressed.

"*I can't* is the only thing that stops us from doing what we're capable of," he said gently. "There's always a way when we have purpose. And our purpose is to reach the other side. Don't worry. Everything is under control. I'll swim with you on my back. First, I'll take your brother. You stay here with the horses, princess. I'll come back for you."

He looked at Blanco and me. "Stay here with her," he said.

"Get on my back," he told Pequeño, who climbed on without hesitation.

My owner bent down, and the boy wrapped his arms around his neck. Blanco and I stood still, watching nervously as they plunged into the river. The current was strong, the water thick with debris, yet Don Felipe swam with the carefree spirit of a child and the strength of a warrior.

Estelita's eyes widened in awe. I understood Blanco, and I felt the same — frozen, stunned, watching him fight the river. He struggled at first but kept going, battling the current dragging him downstream. When he reached the far bank, he set Pequeño down and turned back toward us.

"We are going across," he declared, clearing debris with a large fallen branch.

He untied Blanco and me, urging us forward. We hesitated, fear gripping our hooves. But the fire in his eyes and the calm in his voice gave us courage. Slowly, we stepped into the water. It rose around our legs, then our bellies, until we were swimming.

He led the way, carrying Estelita on his back. At one point, her weight pulled him down, so he kicked harder to stay afloat.

"Dad, Dad, we're sinking!" she cried, panicked. "Daddy! The horses! I can't see them!" she shouted again, her voice rising with fear.

But Blanco and I were strong swimmers. We pushed through the current, even though my heart pounded with uncertainty. I swam with all the boldness I could muster, trusting the river's spirit to guide us.

"They know how to swim! Breathe when you lift your head!" he shouted, his voice steady.

"The current is dragging us!" Estelita cried again.

They surfaced and sank, taking deep breaths between waves. I lost sight of them at times, but finally — soaked, exhausted, and trembling — we broke free of the water's grip and reached the other side.

Relief flooded me. I was nearly fainting, my saddlebags dripping. I took a deep breath — it felt like being born again. Pequeño ran to us, hugging us tightly.

"Oh, my goodness! I was so afraid of drowning," Estelita gasped, pale but safe. "I lost sight of Blanco and Moro. I thought the river had taken them away."

"Good friends, good guys," Don Felipe said, patting our backs. "I'm thrilled we're all safe. Let's dry off before we continue. Hopefully, the sun will warm us up."

Pequeño and my owner wrung out their soaked shirts. Estelita stepped aside, wrapped in a wet towel. The clothes were hung to dry, and the sun — now blazing — quickly did its work. My owner unpacked the saddlebags, shook the water from the supplies, then repacked everything. He helped the children back on.

"Now that everything's ready, let's go!"

We hit the road again, entering the woods beneath towering trees.

"We must go slowly," he warned. "The jungle is fascinating — but also dangerous. Especially for first-timers," he added, glancing at Estelita and me.

He repositioned Blanco after him, and I was following. With each step, our hooves and his footsteps echoed through the jungle.

"Be cautious under the trees," he said, "Watch for wasp hives, low branches, and chonta plants with sharp spikes."

He cleared the way with his machete, slicing through vines and brush. We moved slowly and carefully. Suddenly, Blanco backed away in fear, bumping into me. I stepped back, startled, until Don Felipe grabbed our reins.

"Calm down, boys!"

"Careful! Back up a little more!" he ordered.

"Bend forward as far as you can," he told the children. "Don't move until I say so."

They obeyed. Blanco and I resumed walking, gently pulled forward. I kept my eyes wide, alert. As we passed the spot where Blanco had panicked, I looked up — and froze.

A giant lancehead snake hung from a branch, its head pointed downward, perfectly camouflaged among the leaves. It was so close I could feel its breath. My heart skipped a beat. I didn't want Estelita to see it — she would have screamed. Thankfully, she didn't notice as we passed.

Once the danger had passed, we continued. Estelita was the first to speak.

"Why did we have to bend, Papa?"

Her father revealed that the snake hanging from the branch was an Equis — the most venomous of all snakes.

"Oh, my goodness! It's a giant snake! How scary!" Estelita gasped, her eyes wide with alarm.

She tended to exaggerate when she was scared.

You should have killed it, Dad!

"Kill it? Why would I kill it?" my owner asked calmly.

"Yes, why would he?" Pequeño said, his voice surprisingly honest. He couldn't stand the idea of hurting any creature. "It wasn't hurting us," he added.

"Exactly," my owner affirmed, "All creatures — here in the jungle or anywhere — exist for a reason. Give me only one good reason why I should've killed it," he asked Estelita.

"Well... they're poisonous. You said that one was the most poisonous of all," she replied, unsure.

It is true. Most are venomous but not aggressive. They don't attack unless provoked. Their bite and venom are defensive. In the jungle, many creatures are toxic, but that's how they survive. Nature doesn't make mistakes. Every living being — large, small, or seemingly insignificant — has a purpose. Every brushstroke, shape, and even every scale on a snake belongs exactly where it is. We are all pieces of the grand puzzle of existence — interconnected and part of a whole. Like a drop of the ocean, and the whole ocean, too.

Harming an animal is like hurting yourself because we share the same essence and the same life impulse.

His words carried sincerity and depth. Occasionally, when addressing the children, he would look at Blanco and me —almost as if engaging our very souls. In that moment, I understood his lessons were not just for them, but also meant for us. His composed, straightforward approach awakened something deep inside me. I truly admire and respect him.

He once said, "Only those who live in harmony with nature live a wonderful and dignified life."

After the shock of seeing such a creature, we continue our journey, senses sharp and hearts open. We venture deep into the forest, surrounded by lush greenery. Swarms of bees buzz past my ears, brushing my face as they fly. Others rest in the calyxes of flowers. Birds I'd never seen before flutter and sing, filling the air with music. Wildflowers tremble as I pass, their colors vivid and strange.

The jungle was even more incredible than I had imagined — so much so that I wished I were a poet to describe it. Well… not that I believe there are poets among horses, but who knows? Maybe there are! I chuckled to myself at the thought.

We continue walking, listening to the songs of its creatures, voices telling stories in the wind. Towering, beautiful trees older than time, stretch their roots like tentacles deep into the earth. Their branches hugging each other sway gracefully, and the scent of wildflowers, herbs, wood, and damp soil of that exuberant jungle fills my senses.

We marveled at bromeliads clinging to trunks, orchids in impossible colors, ferns and mosses, and purple bells. Thousands of ants marched along branches, each carrying its load. Grasshoppers fluttered noisily. Ladybugs dotted the leaves. Life was everywhere.

The day was hot and humid, but a gentle breeze and sunlight filtered through the canopy. As we ventured deeper, the jungle grew darker, more fragrant, and more mysterious. Time and space blurred. It felt like another world — because it was.

Sometimes it felt like we were walking in circles, but my owner knew the land like the back of his hand. He moved with ease, confidence, and grace. Lizards darted away like arrows at the sound of our steps. A flock of big bluebirds soared overhead, followed by parrots, quails, doves, partridges, and wild turkeys. Their song filled me with wonder.

Sometimes, silence settled in — vast and endless. No human voice echoed in that paradise except for my owner and his children, who merged with the eternal melody of the jungle.

"Look over there," he said, pointing to a flock of yellow-and-black birds with thick beaks.

"Those are the Dios-te-de tucans — that's what people here call them. They always sing at noon. I've learned to tell time by their songs. Truly, the jungle has been my greatest teacher."

We keep going, amazed.

"Nature is wise," he said, gently pulling on our reins. Then he fell silent, meditative, as if preparing to share something more profound.

Life taught me that we all go through cycles. We are part of a whole. We breathe from the same eternal lung and share the same heartbeat — the rhythm of life.

As the sun began to set, we traveled along a narrow, shadowed path. The closer we got, the more I felt a sense of peace. I listened to the jungle's endless symphony — a place alive with memory, mystery, and meaning. It had existed for centuries and was discovered by my owner long ago.

"We're almost there," he said.

From the ridge, we saw a coffee plantation that stretched like a vast sea of green. I lifted my head to take in the view. With my sharp eyes, I noticed clusters of coffee flowers just starting to bloom, their white petals shining against the leaves. Beyond them were the cacao fields, lush and shadowed.

We stopped there, and my owner, with arms wide open, pointed to a cabin nestled in the heart of it all.

"This is my paradise — my heaven!" he declared with joy. "A place of perfect balance. Do you think there's anywhere better on Earth? I don't. Here, the jungle surrounds us with mystery, exuberance, peace, and serenity. In this place, I feel safe, protected, and loved by everything around me."

His ecstasy was pure, and it overwhelmed me as well. Since I was young, I've been drawn to nature's beauty — its quiet allure and endless wonder.

After we arrived, he helped the children dismount. He unsaddled Blanco and me, then carried the saddlebags to the cabin. Blanco and I wandered into a nearby pasture to graze on fresh grass while the family ate inside.

That night, we slept beneath the magic of a full moon, lulled by the jungle's nocturnal melody.

The next morning, color and light returned, and the jungle came alive again. Birds burst from the trees, filling the sky with their wings and songs.

After breakfast, my owner dressed for work — rubber boots, a straw hat, and a long-sleeved checkered shirt. He grabbed his lunch bag, tucked his machete under his arm, and prepared to head to the coffee and cacao plantation.

The rice harvest has just finished, and now the crops need protection from hungry birds. Don Felipe spread the rice on a large tarp on the ground, and warned the children:

"You two — stay alert. Watch out for the birds. There are hundreds of them, and they'll ruin the harvest quickly. And whatever you do, don't let the rice get wet. If it does, we won't have rice for the whole year. Keep your guard up. Even on a sunny day, storms can appear without warning."

Then he pointed to a group of fluffy chicks, like tiny cotton balls, and issued another warning.

"Keep the chicks away from the pig. She's wild and will eat them if she gets the chance. If she sees them, she'll swallow them whole. Keep the chicks inside the house when she's out. When she's penned, they can roam freely.

Moro, you stay here with the kids."

With that, he mounted Blanco, tipped his hat, and rode toward the plantations. I watched them leave, calm and steady, his hand raised in farewell.

While they left, I stayed grazing by the riverbank, on one side of the hut.

The river flowed softly beneath the willow tree. The plantation shimmered in the distance, and beyond it, the jungle stretched in all its splendor.

The sun beat down on the open area around the cabin. The pig rooted lazily in her sty, and the chicks trailed after their mother, pecking at the ground for food. The sky was bright, and the children exchanged mischievous glances. Then, all at once, they jumped into the river — fully clothed — laughing and shouting as they splashed and dove. Ripples spread across the water. For a moment, it seemed they held the world in their hands.

The heat made me want to join them. I was about to step in when a strong wind blew through the trees. The storm arrived without warning, and the rain began to fall.

"A downpour! Let's get out! The rice is getting wet!" Estelita cried, springing from the water. Pequeño followed, shouting after her.

Then chaos erupted.

The pig had escaped. Pequeño saw her devouring the last chick and burst into tears, shoving her away. Estelita rushed about in a panic, trying to fold the tarp and drag it inside. But the rice was soaked, and the tarp was too heavy to move. The rain poured relentlessly. The harvest was ruined.

The children huddled together, sobbing — not just for the chicks but also out of fear of their father's disappointment.

The air became tense.

Don Felipe returned in a rush, drenched to the bone.

A look of concern crossed his face as he saw them soaking wet, with tears in their eyes. He asked, though he already knew.

"What happened?"

"The pig ate all the chicks," Pequeño said bluntly.

"And the rice got completely soaked…" Estelita added, her voice barely audible.

"Damn it! Didn't I ask you both to take care of the chicks?" He said, his voice tense, his face flushed with concern.

It was the only time I ever saw him so angry.

"Yes," said Pequeño, "but the pig got out of the pen. We had made sure she was inside before we went swimming."

"Swimming?" Don Felipe's voice rose in astonishment. "Didn't I ask you to keep the birds away from the rice and make sure it didn't get wet?"

Estelita was flustered, unable to find the words. At last, calmer now, she admitted it:

"I know… but the sky was so clear, so bright and hot. We didn't expect it to rain. We went swimming, and the storm caught us off guard. Forgive us, dear Daddy," she pleaded, speaking for them both.

At her words, my owner was still frowning — he looked at Estelita with tenderness. He crossed his arms and stared at the horizon for a long time. Then, with a softened expression, he turned to them and said:

"Well… we can't undo what's been done. I hope this teaches you both a lesson. Next time I give instructions, follow them exactly. Do you understand?"

The children nodded, wiping their tears away.

Then he added:

"Sooner or later, every living thing meets its end. That's a truth no one can escape. The lives of those small animals were short. We all go through a cycle and return to nourish the Earth. As the Bible says: '…for dust you are, and to dust shall you return.' "(Genesis 3:19)

"As for the rice, we might not save it, but the birds will enjoy themselves. What I do know is that we'll grow beans and plantains. We won't go hungry."

And with that, the day's chaos settled into silence.

After the storm and the loss of the chicks, with no more duties guarding rice or animals, my owner left Blanco and me with the children while he returned to the plantations. We immediately set out to explore the vast, endless jungle. Even if we walked all day, we'd never reach its edge. Though it was just a grain of sand in the universe, for us it was the entire world.

One day, my owner told the children:

I've only utilized ten hectares for pasture, coffee, and rice, which suffices to sustain us this year and beyond. I will not exploit the remaining land or displace the creatures inhabiting this area.

The jungle balances the Earth, brings rain, and gives life. This is their home. They allow me to farm on their land.

That's how he spoke — to his children, to Blanco, and to me — as if we were his equals.

When it was time to return to the village, we had soaked in its wonders, and its lessons had already taken root in us.

Our journey home slowly took us away from the lush, dreamlike landscape. That morning was peaceful, wrapped in gentle warmth. A soft breeze ruffled our manes. Birds fluttered from branch to branch. We crossed a narrow creek and emerged onto a wide road lined with small houses, their windows painted in bright colors.

Then, in the distance, a herd of horses approached. Among them, a mare caught my eye — her hips swaying rhythmically, her coat gleaming. She was stunning, like a vision. My heart skipped a beat. My breath caught. My mind got clouded, and I lost control.

I forgot Estelita was in my back.

Wild with excitement, I rear up, neighing like a stallion and standing tall on my hind legs.

"Moro, no, no! No!" Estelita screamed, her voice frantic. But I couldn't hear her. I couldn't stop.

"Papa, I'm falling! Papa!" she cried, yanking the reins in desperation. The saddle slipped, sliding toward the ground. I flailed my front legs, trying to impress the mare, blind to everything else.

Stunned, my owner ran toward us.

"Seize control! Take charge!" he shouted.

Estelita's blood ran cold. She couldn't stop me, but everything changed when he reached us.

He grabbed the reins with one hand and slapped my hindquarters with the other. "Epah!" he commanded.

The word echoed through the air like thunder. It was sacred and belonged only to him.

I dropped my legs so fast that the ground trembled beneath me.

Only he could control me in moments like that. What a damn fool I became whenever I saw a mare.

We continued our journey, but this time he placed the bit in my mouth — a punishment I hated. He pulled the reins firmly. I felt his disappointment. He had never used the bit on me before.

One thing was certain: I walked the rest of the way in regret and shame.

After we returned from that first visit to the jungle, the cycles of life kept turning: seasons were born, dawns that flared and faded like tired fireflies.

Estelita and Pequeño left to study in the city.

Meanwhile, my owner, Blanco, and I went each week to tend the plantations. There, we let ourselves be enveloped in his presence, in his care, and in the landscape that stretched before us with rhythm and joy.

8

Melody

On a hot, dusty summer Sunday afternoon, I quietly left the pasture to watch the grazing mares nearby. That's when I saw her — a reddish mare whose eyes met mine like a gentle breeze, stirring my soul.

Her eyes held a brightness that stirred something deep inside me. Her smile — gentle and radiant — filled me with a feeling I couldn't identify. Her gait was graceful, her movements smooth, and suddenly the heat of the day felt pleasant. The world shimmered around me. I felt as if I had levitated, as if I had reached that place they call nirvana or something similar.

The dusk kicked up by my hooves looked like sparkling clouds — fairy dust conjured by invisible wands. Everything around me glowed.

After that first encounter, I couldn't get her out of my mind. The calm in her eyes, the rhythm of her hips, the way her mane fluttered in the breeze — it all held me captive. There was something else as well. A quiet something in her movements, a mystery I couldn't decipher. Yet I was drawn to it. To her.

Blanco looked at me with amusement, likely noticing the goofy expression on my face as I tried my best to neigh, hoping fate would bring her to me. I lost interest in all the other mares. The only one I wanted to see again was her.

I named her Melody — because life felt harmonious when she was near. After hearing the crystal purity of her whinny, the world made more sense. It sounded like music. Like a melody.

From that day on, every weekend, I jumped the fence enclosing my owner's pasture and went in search of the mare who had enchanted me.

Each time I saw her again, a wave of ecstasy washed over me. From that day on, she accepted my love. We strolled together through orange and lemon groves, our hooves brushing the earth in rhythm. Sometimes we chased hummingbirds. Sometimes we stood still, watching the sun sink into the horizon. Often, we were surprised to see the sunrise together.

With her, I felt radiant and luminous. Then nightfall would come, and with it Pequeño, a rope in his hand, ready to take me home.

He'd try to trick me, saying he had salt in one hand. I'd pretend to believe him, not because of the salt, but because I was happy to see him. He never knew how much I loved him.

Even though it hurt to leave Melody, I knew duty was calling. My owner needed me to help with the loads. But I also knew I'd leap the fence again next weekend.

Because Melody was waiting.

9

Goodbye, My Owner, Goodbye!

Winters passed, and summers returned. The bare outlines of dry trees were once again adorned with buds, as life sprouted anew. Flowers faded while others bloomed. Fruits ripened and fell, their seeds giving rise to new plants, sustaining the cycle of life. The moon shifted through its phases, and the Earth spun endlessly around the sun.

And so, three years passed, marked by the rhythm of coming and going between my owner's plantation and the village. That was the last time we walked with him — Blanco and I on the land he loved, savoring the fruits of his labor: coffee, cacao, fruits, grasses... a little of everything the earth chose to give.

During that time, I realized that life is like a big circle, always completing itself. Everything returns to where it started. I observed that when a fruit falls and isn't picked up, it eventually finds its way back to its origin. Each day, nature revealed countless quiet truths to me.

That final weekend, after we reached the village, my owner confided in Doña Felicia that he wished to explore a wild land opposite his plantations. He desired that wild land, thick with vegetation, and he would keep it untouched, a sanctuary where the pulse of nature might remain in balance. Then he added:

"Next time, I'll go with Moro and Blanco to explore."

I remember it was August. Sunflowers along the roadside revealed the month to me. The day was unbearably hot, with the air thick and suffocatingly humid. Before sunrise, the eerie cry of the laughing falcon sent a shiver through me. Blanco raised his head and neighed. I remained still, silent.

The first light of dawn had not yet broken when my owner reached the pasture. He came to fetch us, to take us home before the journey. There, he saddled us up, ready for the journey to explore that new land. His wife helped pack the saddlebags. We carried all the essentials — we would be staying for days.

He placed his hat on his head, tied the ropes to our backs, and said:

We're all set. Let's start the journey before the heat and humidity settle in.

Then he showed us the way and began walking beside us. Sometimes he rode on Blanco, and at other times he rode on my back; we traded the weight between us like a quiet pact. The morning was dim, the air thick, almost humming with its own monotony. My owner, usually talkative, was silent that day; now and then he said something, only to retreat into himself again. It was a little unsettling, yet we continued along the road.

It must have been around noon, and yet the sun had not fully appeared. We had walked for kilometers; we were already growing tired… the place was far away, beneath that dark sky.

"We are nearly there," he said.

We walked another mile or so. Then we heard a thunderous roar, like water crashing through silence. The sound drowned out everything. Soon, we saw it: the Blanco River, named after the whitecaps that broke over the rocks. It was breathtaking. The water sang with life, but to me it was wide, deceptively poetic — fierce, and dangerous.

He took the reins and brought us closer to the water.

"Let's go, buddies! It's not as deep as it looks. Let's cross carefully."

Blanco and I hesitated. We were good swimmers, but the current was the strongest we had ever faced. Still, our owner's determination pushed us forward. We ignored the warning voice horses sometimes hear — a whisper in our soul that tells us something isn't right.

We waded into the water up to our waists. When we tried to back out, he urged us to keep going. Reluctantly, we kept swimming forward. The rocks were jagged, and the current was strong. We stayed alert, avoiding the sharp edges.

"Watch out for the rocks,"

Those were the last words we heard.

A splash. A slip. He fell, hitting his head on a rock. Blood mixed with the water as the current pulled him, tossing him like a rag doll in the foam. He tried to lift his hands, but I think the blow to his head had left him dazed. The river dragged him down, slamming him against the rocks.

Blanco and I were seized by panic.

We rushed out to help him. We neighed with all our strength like two mad creatures while he was being dragged downstream. And before we could do anything, we lost sight of him. It was too late! In the blink of an eye, he was gone. Blanco and I kept neighing at the top of our lungs, but we had to calm down and focus so we could figure out what to do.

Blanco rushed along the riverbank, searching for him, while I, overwhelmed with grief, broke into a frantic run toward his house to call for help.

My blood surged, and my heart felt like it would explode. Dammit! I've never experienced such fear.

I lunged forward like never before, soaring through the air, overwhelmed by sorrow. The saddlebag flew away. The endless road ahead seemed to stretch on forever. I was soaked in sweat, my heart heavy with grief.

Nearly out of breath, I burst into the yard with frantic kicks, knocking down the fence and crashing against the house walls in a frenzy. I felt hopeless and shattered.

Doña Felicia appeared, startled by the chaos.

She didn't understand my frantic kicks or desperate cries. She tried to calm me as she looked for the rope.

"Easy, Moro, easy!"

My reaction was so out of character that she didn't understand. I ran away as fast as I could, then bolted back to the house, pounding my hooves and wallowing in my misery over the pain I felt for my poor owner.

Damn it! That was a moment in my life when I wished I could speak human language.

She tried to grab the rope again.

"Easy, boy, easy!"

But I couldn't calm down. I neighed urgently, paced in circles, stomped, trembling. My eyes pleaded for her to realize — something awful had occurred. She paused, her face turning more serious than worried. Her expression shifted. She let go of the rope.

"What's wrong, Moro? Where is he?" she shouted.

There was no time to lose.

"Help! Someone help me!" she shouted with all her might.

One of the neighbors ran toward her. I finally stopped when she called for help.

"What's wrong?" the neighbor asked.

Something happened to Felipe. In the morning, he went out with the horses, and now Moro has come by itself and is out of control. I stopped when she understood it.

I'm heading there, please tell my boys the bad news.

She climbed to ride. I turned and galloped towards the trail, and soon the news had spread like wildfire. Others joined us on their horses. We raced together, along the path, back toward the river, the air thick with dread, and the road seemed eternal.

When we reached the riverbank, the river had quieted a bit, but its song remained just as harsh.

Doña Felisa dropped to her knees, repeatedly calling his name.

"Felipe! Where are you? Answer me."

Only silence.

Sadness hung in the air.

Along the river, rescue teams in canoes were working; others were on horseback, and, just like me, Doña Felicia and I hurried downstream, desperate to find him. After hours of searching, the shadows of night took over; darkness settled around us. Some lit lamps and flashlights to illuminate the way.

Then, in the silence, a man shouted. "Here is Don Felipe's body." Two men brought his body ashore. I lifted my head toward the light. And I stepped back to let them pass.

Far downstream, they discovered him tangled in reeds near the bend. Blanco was next to him, his coat soaked and eyes wild. He whinnied upon seeing us and circled the water's edge.

His body was broken, his hat tangled next to his head, as if reluctant to let go of the man it had shaded for so many years. The river had taken him, but it hadn't hidden him. Instead, it returned him — battered, silent, yet recognizable enough to be mourned.

On the way home, the night was filled with mourning. I felt profound emptiness and loss. Doña Felicia silently wept, tears streaming down her face. Blanco and I walked nearby, heads bowed, tails still, hearts broken.

When we arrived, we had to push through the crowd so the men carrying him could enter his house.

"We must make arrangements for the funeral," Doña Felicia said softly, her voice heavy with sorrow.

Friends and family moved quickly. Within an hour, everything was ready for the wake.

The coffin was placed in the center of the room, surrounded by flickering candles. Across from it, women dressed in mourning knelt in prayer, some quietly weeping, others sobbing aloud.

That night, the entrance by the avocado tree fell silent. No laughter, no footsteps, only the soft rustle of trees and the distant cry of a mourning dove.

Soon, the three teens arrived.

Their screams cut through the air.

"No!" screamed Estelita. "Dad… Dad… my dear daddy, please don't go!"

She mourned the loss of his eternal love, his wisdom, and his laughter. Tears streamed down her cheeks.

"You can't be dead! It must be a mistake! How could he drown when he swam like a fish?"

The three enveloped her mother, their grief profound and silent. As they wept, a hurricane of sorrow tore through me, making my body shiver uncontrollably. Life without him would never be the same. With him, I had lived in a dreamland. I had everything. As the young ones say, I was set.

Their cries merged with Blanco's and mine as we mourned together, our spirits unraveling. We tried to escape the pain by holding onto memories — his voice, his touch, and the rhythm of our shared days.

Estelita stood beside the coffin, her eyes distant and unfocused. Tears fell silently, and her shadow flickered like candlelight. I watched her from outside, through the window. Her silhouette moved mysteriously, like my reflection trembling over the river on a moonlit night.

I didn't sleep. I stood by the fence, staring at the stars and wondering whether he had become one of them. Blanco lay beside me, his breathing slow and his spirit dimmed.

The next day was his funeral.

We reached his final resting place under a calm, clear sky — quiet, as his life had been. White clouds drifted overhead as the casket was carried to the cemetery.

As it was lowered into the ground, Pequeño threw the first handful of dirt, his voice trembling.

"Goodbye, Papa. You will no longer share your wisdom with me. You have let me become an orphan of your love."

Estelita and her mother cried uncontrollably. But when the first shovel of earth was dumped, Estelita grew still. She kissed a flower from her bouquet and gently placed it on the coffin.

"Life is like the fleeting flight of a passing bird," she whispered, echoing her father's words. *"Today we are happy here; tomorrow, we may be in the grave. That's why we must live joyfully, content with ourselves."*

As the grave was fully covered and we prepared to leave, two beautiful birds soared overhead, circling as if to say a final goodbye.

On the way home, wrapped in silence… with every step, I missed him.

The birds will no longer sing to you in your sky: my beloved, you have fallen to become the fruit that sustains. But your laughter remains hanging: an echo in the forest, a whisper in the wind, a silence in every path you crossed. Every dawn you beheld stayed with your memory, a blessing for having seen you and for waiting for you… in eternity, in all, in nothing. As your body becomes fertile earth, filled with fruit and fragrance, you will travel through time with your voice and laughter: an eternal melody.

10

Ashes

After the burial, the children embraced us once more — their hugs weighed with grief — before heading back to their studies in the city. Blanco and I then wandered tirelessly, both day and night, unable to escape the pain. Occasionally, feeling drained and restless, we would burst into frantic races, galloping across the fields in a desperate attempt to escape the ache within.

But the memories clung to us. They pulled at my heart like reins — soft, persistent reminders of the days when he was still with us.

In the house, his empty space was filled with grief. The animals missed
his laughter,
his kindness,
his love.

Time passed, and so did life.

Doña Felicia sold the jungle crops and the house in the village. She moved to the city to live with her children, who were now in college. Blanco and I found food in Melody's pasture or in other fields, where we were always welcomed. But nothing felt the same.

One day, Blanco and I returned to the jungle — to the land that once belonged to our owner. The water was clear. The grass was plentiful. It felt like home. We could sense his soul in the air.

We stayed for days in his cherished spot, which he considered his paradise, where he would sit for hours, lost in thought. I couldn't grasp Blanco's feelings, but I could sense his presence everywhere — in the whispering wind, the singing birds, the murmuring river, the glowing flowers, and every star that guided us. In the sunset, in the sunrise, in the noisy jungle, and in the silence.

The night gradually darkened. The moon, low and obscured by clouds — ashen and distant among the trees — seemed to mourn as well. Even the river, pale and silent, shimmered with nostalgia.

At dawn the air felt thick and suffocating. The silent forest was broken by the zigzagging movements of birds and monkeys gathering, sensing danger in the air.

Then we heard it — a rumble.

The earth trembled, seemingly sinking beneath me. I whinnied in fear as birds darted away in a flurry, alarmed by the thunderous sound through the forest. Then, the trees came crashing down in a violent cascade.

Chaos erupted.

We saw men cutting down trees and setting them on fire.

We moved swiftly and chaotically, evading falling trunks, jumping over roots, and whimpering in fear. Blanco pointed the way, and I followed. Flames licked the air. Smoke curled around us. We raced at full speed, weaving back and forth to dodge falling trees and the intense heat of the fire, desperately searching for an escape.

We kept running, powerless to stop the destruction. Finally, we reached a clearing, slightly less crowded, and escaped the inferno.

The noise was deafening.

The earth groaned as ancient trees collapsed. Birds, stunned and frightened, fell from their branches. The vibrant voices of canaries, bluebirds, toucans, and parrots fell silent, leaving the jungle in a painful weeping. Small and large animals fled from their homes. The wind howled fiercely, intensifying the flames.

And paradise turned to ash.

The heat was suffocating, and our eyes flickered and shimmered with smoke. The atmosphere was heavy, suffocating the animals, who were neither crushed nor burned by the flames but were stunned. There was no escape. Branches burst into flames like torches, and the once lively soundscape of the jungle gradually fell silent. Life was being extinguished amid the noise of axes, chainsaws, and flames.

The fire kept consuming everything.

We finally escaped and took refuge at a nearby farm. That night, we couldn't sleep and remained filled with grief. Even there, the leaves curled from the heat, and smoke hung in the air like a ghost that refused to leave.

By the following evening, we quietly returned to the ruined site.

The Earth, scorched and broken, seemed to weep. Once fragrant, it now reeked of burnt death. As I looked around, pain overwhelmed me. Tears filled my eyes. Nothing remained. The crops my owner had tended were gone. No birds crossed the sky. No ants carried leaves. No lizards darted past my steps. Not a ladybug. Not a seed to grow, not a whisper of life.

Everything had been destroyed.

Ashes blanketed the ground where the trees once stood. The cries of desperate animals echoed in my mind, and my heart ached. My pupils dilated, haunted by the final moments of those with no escape.

That night, no fireflies lit the darkness, and no frogs sang their nighttime lullaby. The silence was complete.

I tried to understand. What had happened? What were those men thinking? Why destroy a forest that had nurtured life for generations? My questions hung in the air, unanswered, like smoke that refused to clear.

Blanco and I stood quietly, our hearts heavy. I felt a shadow within me, as if I were trapped in a nightmare I couldn't wake from. Sadness and exhaustion wrapped around me. The images of destruction haunted me, making me shiver each time they returned. I looked into Blanco's eyes, but he was also lost in sorrow. That only deepened my own.

After one final glance at the destruction, I communicated with my friend — not with words, but through my eyes.

Let's go, Blanco. There's nothing else to do here.

And so, quietly, we walked away from the place that had once been my owner's paradise.

Now, it was just an ocean of ash.

11

A New Life

As we left the jungle ruins behind, Blanco and I slowly climbed the hill, our hearts heavy with nostalgia. We wandered from place to place, retracing our steps, each step worn by memory, until exhaustion settled over us like a blanket of dust.

The days passed relentlessly.

We visited the pasture, the quiet corners where he once stood. We passed the house that had belonged to him — now empty, its fence fallen, Doña Felicia's Garden withering. One afternoon, I saw Verde descend the avocado tree, his movements slow and sorrowful. Linda stood nearby, contemplative and still. Giro, Pancho the pig, and the others were nowhere to be found. Perhaps they had met the fate of those considered delicious and nutritious. That thought stung, but I knew it was probably true.

On one of those melancholy days, we wandered back to the pasture. A gentle breeze brushed against me, making me shiver. I felt him — his presence, soft and familiar — as if his arms were wrapping around my neck, just as they used to. Then came his voice, not loud but clear, echoing through my mind like a sacred whisper.

Moro… don't be sad. Death is part of life. It's not the end — it's a beginning. Every time a flower falls, a new one is born. Sadness and joy are sisters. Happiness lives in your conscience. Live, Moro. You're not truly alive if you're not happy. Find satisfaction. You still have so much: Blanco's friendship, Melody's love, beautiful memories, and the world around you. Even if Estelita and Pequeño seem distant, they carry you in their hearts. They'll return. Everything you've endured was necessary. Don't let sorrow consume you.

When humans wake from the dream of unconsciousness, they will respect the earth, its creatures, and the life that sustains us. Until then, destruction will continue. But don't worry — life flows like a river. It lives, it dies, it renews. I haven't abandoned you. I live in your heart. Don't wait for others to change. The only change you can trust is the one within yourself.

I believe Blanco heard it too. His eyes lit up, and something shifted in his expression — as if a cloud lifted.

It felt as if spring had quietly arrived.

My heart began to bloom again. I thought, it's true. He hasn't left me. He's in everything I learned from him, in every act of love, and above all, he's alive in my heart.

We picked up speed, our steps lighter. I looked up at the sky — oh! What a spectacle! Amethyst, rose, and soft hues shimmered above us, refracted by the quartz and crystals in the earth. The air was warm and gentle.

We jumped over the fence into Melody's pasture. A friendly, old woman saw us and smiled. "You can stay with me; you keep me company," she told us. Her wrinkled hand drifted gently over our coats with a tenderness that felt almost ethereal. In her gentle, generous voice, I heard an echo of Doña Felicia, distant, familiar, impossible to forget. Trusting her, I rested my head on her shoulder. Her presence — calm, loving, like a gentle breeze — lifted us from the sadness that had been holding us down.

Something was changing. The air felt soothing. The fields began to bloom. Birds sang again, sweeter than ever. I had passed the winter of my grief; it was over, and spring had returned — not just in nature, but within me.

Everything turned green again.

Everything became music and poetry.

Flowers released their fragrance like a hymn.

Fascinated by the scenic view and the gentle flow of life, I drifted into memory. Bright afternoons returned to me — filled with the laughter of two children who had once entered my world like a miracle. And we would run together through green fields scented with ambrosia, their joy contagious. I sank into the warmth of red hibiscus, colorful bougainvillea, hazel-toned beehives, fresh greenery, laughter, and fantasy.

That day, longing bloomed within me. I welcomed the hope of seeing them again. I refused to believe they were gone forever.

As I stood in quiet contemplation, surrounded by beauty, I heard two familiar voices — music to my ears.

"Moro," they called, running toward me.

I lifted my head, feeling my mane catch the wind. Overwhelmed with joy, I was unsure if it was reality or a dream fueled by longing. But it was truly real — wonderfully so. I galloped over, whinnying with delight. Their eyes shone brightly, and a sense of spring blossomed in me again. We embraced warmly as Blanco ran toward us, his excitement heightening our happiness. The four of us reveled in that joyful reunion.

Pequeño — though the nickname no longer suited him, and he no longer carried a rope the way he used to, ready to lead me away — came this time with a sheet of paper to draw us. While he worked and tried to keep me still, I, mischievous as ever, danced around him the way I always did. Time has passed, and he is no longer the little boy who once found me in someone else's pasture. He had grown into a sensitive young man eager to capture the beauty of life on canvas.

We spent the afternoon together. After hugging Blanco, Melody, and me, they left, promising to return. And they did, throughout our lives.

That night, a warm wind swept along the path. The creek flowed peacefully, its waters singing a gentle tune. Blossoms lined the flower–filled trail, their scent carried by the breeze. My heart was calm and serene. Fireflies shimmered like fallen stars beneath the moonlight, among violets and jasmine.

At dawn, the rooster crowed. By the orchard, near fragrant orange groves, Melody's cry rang out — a sound of new life.

A colt was born.

So tender, so soft. A gift from life itself. Melody cleaned and warmed him. When he stood on his four legs, he confidently searched for his teat. We named him Morito — little Moro.

Later that morning, across the pasture, Morito watched a hummingbird chase a fluttering butterfly. Melody, Blanco, and I watched, entertained, and enchanted.

On both sides of the pasture, trees stood tall, bathed in golden sunlight. Wild violets peeked from dew–covered grass. In the distance, flowers of every color danced in the wind. Beyond them, infinity faded into light.

As I remembered my owner, the great master of my life, I felt I loved the whole universe; through him, I was infused with its fragrance, its colors, and its soul.

I let the sun caress me.

And I choose happiness, just as he did.

The End.

Epilogue

Though this story is told from the point of view of a remarkable horse named *Moro*, it is based on real events.

The journey you've read truly happened. The main characters: two horses — Moro and Blanco — two children, Estelita and Pequeño; and their parents, Don Felipe and Doña Felicia — were part of a life shaped by nature, love, and loss.

Even the moments that seemed unbelievable — the force of the river, crossing it on her father's back, the destruction of the magical land he called paradise, his final attempt to swim across the Blanco river, Moro's frantic race for help, and Blanco's quiet vigil beside Don Felipe's body — are all true.

Time and love have only deepened Moro's presence in the hearts of those who lived this nature–born adventure. His story remains vibrant — a tribute to loyalty, to the Earth, and to the enduring spirit of those who never truly leave us.

May this story remind you that memory is a kind of immortality, and love, when rooted in truth, never fades.

"Faster, faster, faster!" they cheered.

We pushed through the current even though my heart
pounded with uncertainty.

93

"Seize control! You have the reins!"

Nearly out of breath, I burst into the yard with frantic kicks.

We named him Morito — little Moro.

9 789899 551681